the it girl

CREATED BY

CECILY VON ZIEGESAR

SNEAK PEEK!
Preview chapters from
this hot new novel

Available Now

LITTLE, BROWN AND COMPANY

New York ❧ Boston ❧ London

Copyright © 2005 by Alloy Entertainment

Little, Brown and Company

Time Warner Book Group
1271 Avenue of the Americas, New York, NY 10020
Visit our Web site at www.lb-teens.com

First Edition: November 2005

 Produced by Alloy Entertainment
151 West 26th Street, New York, NY 10001

SAMPLER ISBN 0-316-15481-4

10 9 8 7 6 5 4 3 2 1
CWO
Printed in the United States of America

A WAVERLY OWL DOES NOT DISCUSS

HALF-NAKEDNESS WITH STRANGERS.

Somebody's plaid Jack Spade duffel slammed into Jenny Humphrey's shin and jerked her out of a dream. The 10 A.M. Amtrak Empire Service to Rhinecliff, New York, had stopped in Poughkeepsie, and a tall, twentyish, stubbly chinned boy in dark brown square Paul Smith glasses and a Decemberists T-shirt was standing over her.

"Anybody sitting here?" he asked.

"Nope," she responded groggily, scooting over. He threw his bag under the seat and settled in next to Jenny.

The train groaned along at about a mile an hour. Jenny sniffed at the stale, slightly sweaty train car air and jiggled her foot, thinking about how she was going to be super-late for check-in at Waverly Academy. She would've been early if her dad, Rufus, had driven her up here in his blue beater Volvo wagon—he'd practically begged Jenny to let him—but Jenny hadn't wanted her unshaven, peacenik father to drop her off at her brand-new, haute boarding school. Knowing him, he'd have tried to start up an impromptu poetry slam with her new class-mates and shown off old pictures of Jenny when she was a lame seventh grader and wore nothing but fluorescent green and orange Old Navy fleeces. Um, no thanks.

"Going to Waverly?" the boy asked. He raised his eyebrows at the *Waverly Academy Guide to Ethics* that sat unopened in Jenny's lap.

Jenny brushed a brown tendril out of her eyes. "Yeah," she answered. "I'm starting there this year." She couldn't hide the enthusiasm in her voice—she was so excited to start her brand-new boarding school that she felt all jiggly inside, like she had to pee.

"Freshman?"

"Nope. Sophomore. I used to go to Constance Billard. It's in the city." Jenny was a little pleased that she had a relatively chic past to refer to, or that it at least sounded that way.

"So you wanted a change of pace, or what?" He fiddled with the strap of his worn leather watchband.

Jenny shrugged. This boy looked like he was her brother Dan's age. Dan had just taken off for Evergreen College on the West Coast two days ago, taking nothing with him except for two duffel bags, his Mac G4 laptop, and two cartons of ciga-rettes. Jenny, on the other hand, had already shipped four over-size boxes and a couple of giant duffels to Waverly, and had lugged a giant suitcase and an overstuffed bag with her. In her hyperexcited preparation for boarding school, she had practically bought out the hair, cosmetics, and feminine products aisles at CVS—who knew what she'd need at boarding school! She'd also gone on a buying spree at Club Monaco, J.Crew, and Barneys with the credit card her dad had lent her for back-to-school shopping. "Kinda," she finally answered.

The truth was, she'd been asked to leave Constance—apparently because she was considered a "bad influence" on the other girls. Jenny hadn't thought she was being a bad influence at all—she was just trying to have fun, like every other girl at school. But somehow, all of her moments of extreme fun had also been highly publicized and embarrassing: a picture of her boobs in a sports bra had shown up in a magazine (she'd thought it was a sportswear model shoot), a Webcast of her practically naked butt had been spread around the school, and she'd made some bad decisions about which boys she should make out with at various parties—and of course everybody had found out.

The final straw had come after Jenny had spent a night at the Plaza Hotel with her brother's old band, the Raves. A photograph of her leaving the Plaza in nothing but a fluffy white bathrobe had appeared online on Page Six the next day. Rumors had flown that Jenny was sleeping with *all* the Raves, *including* her brother. Ew! Concerned parents quickly called up the Constance headmistress, aflutter about Jenny's promiscuity. After all, Constance had a reputation for excellence to uphold!

Although Jenny hadn't even been with *one* Rave, let alone all of them, she hadn't exactly wanted to *deny* the rumor—she kind of loved that everyone was talking about her. So as she'd sat with the Constance Billard headmistress, Ms. McLean, in her patriotic red, white, and blue office back in the city, Jenny had realized something huge: it wasn't the end of the world to get kicked out of Constance. This was her chance to start over, to reinvent herself as the blunder-free sophisticate she'd always wanted to be. And where was the classiest place to start over? Boarding school, of course.

Much to her dad's chagrin—she was pretty sure Rufus wanted her to live with him in their Upper West Side apartment forever—Jenny had rabidly researched a whole bunch of schools and toured a few. The first school had turned out to have a strict disciplinary code and had been too boring for words. Within minutes of getting to the second school, on the other hand, she'd been offered Ecstasy and had taken her top off. But just like the third bed for Goldilocks, the third school that Jenny had tested, Waverly, was just right.

Well, to tell the truth, she hadn't actually visited Waverly— she'd run out of time, applied way past the deadline, and taken some creative liberties with her application—but she'd looked at thousands of pictures online and memorized all the building names and campus maps. She was certain it would be perfect.

"I used to go to Waverly's rival," the boy said, pulling a book out of his bag. "St. Lucius. Our school hated your school."

"Oh," Jenny replied quietly, sinking into her seat.

"I'm kidding." He smiled and turned back to his book. Jenny noticed it was Henry Miller's *Tropic of Cancer*, one of her dad's favorites. According to Rufus, it had been banned because it was too right-on in its vicious social commentary about love and sex in New York City. Hello, sex scenes. Jenny felt her cheeks growing pink.

Then she realized: she was acting like her old, unsophisticated self. And one thing was for sure: Old Jenny obviously wasn't working for her.

Jenny studied the boy carefully. She didn't know him and would probably never see him again, so why did she care what he thought of her? At Waverly, Jenny was going to be stunning, amazing New Jenny, the girl who belonged at the center of everything.

So why not become New Jenny starting *right now?*

Mustering up her courage, she uncrossed her arms to reveal her rather large double-D chest, which seemed even bigger, since she was barely five feet tall, and sat up straight. "So, um, any good parts in that book?"

The boy looked puzzled, his eyes darting back and forth from Jenny's innocent face to her chest to the worn paperback's cover. Finally, he wrinkled his nose and answered, "Maybe."

"Will you read some to me?"

The boy licked his lips. "Okay. But only if you read me a line from that book you've got there first." He tapped the maroon cover of her beloved *Waverly Academy Guide to Ethics.*

"Sure." Jenny opened the rule book. She'd received it a few weeks ago and had devoured it cover to cover. She loved its plush leather binding, its creamy paper stock, and the nursery-rhymey, slightly condescending, slightly British style in which it was written. It sounded so wonderfully proper and upscale, and Jenny was sure that by the time she'd even spent a few weeks at Waverly, she'd be as polished, graceful, and perfect as Amanda Hearst, the young socialite, or the late Carolyn Bessette Kennedy.

She cleared her throat. "Here's a good one. 'Waverly Owls may not dance in a sexually suggestive manner in public.'" She laughed. Did that mean they could dance in a sexually suggestive manner in *private*?

"Do they really refer to you as Waverly Owls?" The boy leaned over to look at the page. He smelled like Ivory soap.

"Yes!" As she said it, Jenny grinned. She, Jenny Humphrey, was going to be a Waverly Owl!

She turned the page. "'Waverly Owls are not permitted sexual intimacy. A Waverly Owl must not engage in activities that might be dangerous, such as jumping off the Richards Bridge. A Waverly Owl does not wear spaghetti straps or miniskirts above midthigh.'"

The boy snickered. "When they're talking about a girl, shouldn't it be an Owlette?"

Jenny slammed the book shut. "Okay. Now it's your turn."

"Well, I just started, so I'll read from the beginning." The boy smirked and opened to the first page. "'From the very beginning, I have trained myself not to want anything too badly.'"

Funny, Jenny thought. She had the opposite problem—she wanted everything *way* too badly.

"'I was corrupt,'" he continued. "'Corrupt from the start.'"

"I'm corrupt!" Jenny blurted out. "But not from the start." Old Jenny couldn't believe what New Jenny was saying.

"Yeah?" He closed the book. "I'm Sam, by the way."

"Jenny." She looked down to see if Sam wanted her to shake his hand, but it was still wedged under his leg. They both smiled awkwardly.

"So, does your corruptness have anything to do with why you're leaving New York for boarding school?" Sam asked.

"Maybe." Jenny shrugged, trying to be coy and mysterious at the same time.

"Spill."

She let out a sigh. She could admit the truth, but *Everybody thought I was sleeping with all the guys in this band, and I didn't deny it* sounded kind of slutty. Definitely not mysterious or chic. So instead she decided to take some creative liberties. "Well, I was in a sort of risqué fashion show."

Sam's eyes glittered with interest. "What do you mean?"

She thought for a moment. "Well, for one look, I just had this bra-and-underwear set on. And heels. I guess it was a little too much for some people."

This wasn't entirely a lie. Jenny *had* modeled last year—for a Les Best spread in *W* magazine. Clothed. But clothes didn't seem too interesting at the moment.

"Really?" Sam cleared his throat and readjusted his glasses. "Have you heard of Tinsley Carmichael? You should know her."

"Who?"

"Tinsley Carmichael. She goes to Waverly. I go to Bard now, but I met her a couple times at parties last year. . . . She came to school in her own seaplane. But someone told me she decided to leave Waverly because Wes Anderson offered her the lead in his next movie."

Jenny shrugged, feeling strangely competitive with—and a wee bit excited about—this Tinsley girl. She sounded like the ideal New Jenny.

The exhausted-looking train conductor stomped down the aisle and grabbed the ticket off the top of her seat. "Rhinecliff, next."

"Oh. This is me." Jenny took a deep breath. It was really happening! She looked out the window, expecting to see something truly magical, but saw only lush green trees, a wide field, and telephone poles. Still, trees! A field! The only field in Manhattan was Sheep Meadow in Central Park, and it was always filled with drug dealers and really skinny half-naked girls sunbathing.

She stood and reached for her red and white polka-dotted soft-shell LeSportsac bag and the old-school brown Samsonite suitcase she'd borrowed from her dad. It had a big HUGS NOT BOMBS sticker next to the handles. Not very New Jenny. As she struggled to bring the case to the ground, Sam stood to help her, pulling it effortlessly off the rack.

"Thanks," she said, blushing.

"No problem." He pushed the hair out of his eyes. "So, do I get to see pictures of you at . . . at the fashion show?"

"If you search online," Jenny lied. She stared out the window and saw, across a field, an old rooster weathervane on the top of a large, faded farmhouse. "The designer's name is, um, Rooster."

"Never heard of him."

"He's kind of obscure," Jenny answered quickly, noting that

the polished, pink Polo wearing boy sitting behind them was definitely listening to their conversation. Jenny tried to see what he was typing on his BlackBerry, but he covered the screen when he noticed her watching him.

"You . . . you should come to Bard sometime," Sam continued. "We have some killer parties. Great DJs and stuff."

"Okay," Jenny replied over her shoulder, raising her eyebrows just a touch. "Although, you know, a Waverly Owl isn't allowed to dance in a sexually suggestive manner."

"I won't tell on you," he answered, not taking his eyes off her chest.

"'Bye, Sam," Jenny waved, using her most flirty, musical voice. She stepped off the train onto the platform and sucked in a deep breath of fresh country air. *Whoa.*

New Jenny would take a little getting used to!

RyanReynolds: Hey, Benster. Welcome back, girl!

BennyCunningham: Hey, sweetie! How's life?

RyanReynolds: I had the worst ride up here in our plane. My dad has this maniac pilot and they were yakking at each other the whole time and going faster and faster. . . .

BennyCunningham: Next time you should fly with me. I'll let you snuggle with me under my pashmina.

RyanReynolds: God, you're a tease. Hey, did u c Callie's pic in Atlanta Magazine?

BennyCunningham: No, but I heard it nearly ruined her mom. She had to do damage control on Good Morning Atlanta!

RyanReynolds: Yeah, C looks bombed in the pic.

BennyCunningham: Is she still with EZ? I'm going to jump him if she's not.

RyanReynolds: Dunno. Someone told me they saw him dancing with some gorgeous girl with really blue eyes and black dreads in Lexington.

BennyCunningham: Sorta sounds like Tinsley. Except for the dreads.

RyanReynolds: I know. Too bad she won't be at the party tonight.

BennyCunningham: Seriously.

A WAVERLY OWL SHOULD RESIST THE URGE
TO LICK HER BOYFRIEND FROM HEAD TO TOE.

Callie Vernon set her luggage down in the entranceway to Dumbarton dorm room 303 and looked around. The room was exactly as she, Brett, and Tinsley had left it—except for the lack of empty Diet Coke bottles, Parliament butt–filled ashtrays, and CD cases strewn all over the room. Last fall, because they'd only been sophomores, Callie and her two best friends, Brett Messerschmidt and Tinsley Carmichael, had been assigned a horrible, cramped room with only one window. But then Tinsley had bribed three dorky senior girls to switch with them the first week of school by promising them invites to the best secret parties. They'd wanted this room because it was bigger than most, with casement windows overlooking the Hudson River, and because it was close to the fire escape—ideal for sneaking out after curfew.

Brett hadn't arrived back at school yet, and Tinsley had been expelled at the end of school last year. They'd been caught on Ecstasy in the middle of the rugby fields at five in the morning by Mr. Purcell, the uptight physics teacher, who liked going running with his three impeccably groomed giant schnauzers before sunrise. It was the first time they'd ever tried E, and it had taken them a moment to stop laughing at the ridiculous-looking dogs before realizing what enormous trouble they were in. The girls had all been called into the headmaster's office separately—first Tinsley, then Callie, then Brett—but the only one to get in any real trouble was Tinsley, who was promptly booted out of Waverly.

Callie caught a glimpse of herself in the just-Windexed mirror over the antique oak bureau and straightened her white Jill Stuart shell top and pleated lemon-yellow Tocca skirt. She'd lost a few pounds over the summer and the side zipper kept sliding around to her belly button. Callie was thin now, maybe a little too thin, and freckly from the summer. Her hair was long and shaggy, and her round, hazel eyes were fanned by thick, blond-tipped eyelashes. She puckered her lips, blew a kiss at the mirror, and felt an anxious flutter in her chest.

All this summer, Callie's mind had spun, thinking about why Tinsley had been expelled and she and Brett hadn't been. Had Brett set it up that way? Brett was supersecretive about her life at home—her mom and dad never came to Parents' Day, and Brett never invited anybody to her house in East Hampton for long weekends. Tinsley had once dropped a hint that Brett had some family issues she didn't want anybody to know about.

Could Brett really have orchestrated Tinsley's expulsion so she wouldn't expose her secrets? It sounded totally soap-operaish, but Brett was so melodramatic sometimes that Callie wouldn't put it past her.

Callie nestled into her desk chair, actually glad to be back at school. Beyond not talking to her two best friends—she hadn't heard a peep from either of them—her summer had been a disaster. First, there'd been the *Atlanta Magazine* photo of Callie at Club Compound, dancing on a table with a vanilla martini in her hand. The caption read, *Overserved and underage: Is this appropriate behavior for a governor's daughter?* Needless to say, that hadn't gone over well with her mother's conservative Georgian voters. Oops.

After that nightmare, Callie had flown to her family's chalet in Barcelona—Mr. Vernon was part Spanish and spent his summers working on real estate deals in Europe. She had hoped that Barcelona would be the perfect backdrop for a romantic rendezvous with her boyfriend, Easy Walsh. But that visit had been anything but romantic. Try freaky.

"Hey," came a gravelly voice behind her.

Callie wheeled around. Easy. There he was, all rumpled, sexy six feet of him, standing in her doorway, looking more gorgeous than ever.

"Oh!" She felt her palms get slick with sweat.

"How are you?" he asked, pulling at the worn hem of his polo shirt. His glossy almost-black hair curled around his neck and ears.

"Confused" would have been a reasonable answer. The last

time she'd seen Easy was when she'd dropped him off at the Barcelona airport. They hadn't kissed goodbye, and they'd barely even spoken the whole last day of his visit.

"Fine," she replied cautiously. "How did you get in here? Did Angelica see you?" Her dorm mistress, Angelica Pardee, was really strict about allowing boys in the all-girls' dorm except during "visitation," which was only for an hour between sports practice and dinner.

"You look too skinny," Easy said softly, ignoring Callie's questions.

Callie frowned. "Do you want to get in trouble on the first day of school?"

"Your boobs are going away," he continued.

"God," she muttered in annoyance. The truth was, she hadn't been hungry all summer—not even for Barcelona-style paella, her favorite. She was too nervous to eat, or to do much of anything, really. The last few weeks in Spain she'd spent on the couch, looking like an unstructured slob, wearing her slightly ragged, white Dior string bikini and some old ripped batik sarong she'd picked up for next to nothing in a Barcelona outdoor market, watching hours and hours of *The Surreal Life* in Spanish. And she didn't even speak much Spanish. "What are you doing back so soon?"

Easy was usually fashionably late to Waverly check-in— another no-no—because he arrived in a tractor-trailer with his Thoroughbred, Credo, who he kept on campus.

"Credo's coming next week, so there was no reason for me to be late."

He looked at Callie. They'd been together since last fall, but he'd had a hard time getting psyched to see her back at school after his parents had received an angry note from Dean Marymount over the summer saying he'd be watching Easy carefully this year. Apparently there were rules to uphold, and just because Easy was a legacy—his grandfather, father, and three older brothers had all attended Waverly—didn't mean he could bend those rules. So instead of heading up to school a week late with Credo, Easy had flown alone on a chartered plane from Kentucky to New York with leather reclining seats and unlimited champagne. Sounds great, right? Except it wasn't exactly what Easy had had in mind.

Easy regularly fantasized about getting kicked out of Waverly Academy—until he remembered his father's bargain. If Easy graduated from Waverly, he could take a postgraduate year in Paris. His father even had a big apartment in the Latin Quarter all ready for Easy's year abroad. Paris—how cool would that be? He'd drink absinthe, paint street scenes from his bedroom window, and ride along the Seine on an ancient, rickety Peugeot bike, a Gauloise hanging from his mouth. He could smoke his brains out and nobody would give him shit for it!

"You going to the party at Richards' lounge tonight?" Callie asked.

Easy shrugged. "Not sure." He stood just inside the door frame.

Callie pulled a foot out of her pointy-toed Burberry loafer and rolled her ballerina-pink painted toes against the floor. A horrible feeling of dread washed over her. *Why* wouldn't Easy want to go to the first party of the year? *Everybody* went to the first party of the year. Was he seeing someone else? Someone he wanted to be alone with on the first night of school?

"Well, I'm going," she said quickly, crossing her arms.

Neither one had made a move toward the other. But with his mussed hair, broad shoulders, and golden-brown forearms, Easy looked so irresistible, Callie was dying to lick him from head to toe.

"Did you have a good summer after Spain?" she squeaked, trying to sound as indifferent as possible.

"I guess. Lexington was ass-boring as usual." He pulled a toothpick from behind his ear and placed it between his slightly chapped lips.

Callie leaned against her antique white-painted wood bed frame. His visit to Spain had been tainted from the start. Easy had had to fly coach class, and when he'd arrived, he'd been terse and gruff and had headed straight to the bar—not one of those cute little outdoor cafés straight out of *The Sun Also Rises*, but simply the closest bar possible, at the airport. Then he'd passed out on the Vernons' couch, which was a real problem since Callie's dad *needed* to sit on that couch to watch the international feed of CNN every single minute he wasn't working.

Callie tilted her hips forward and chewed on her freshly manicured thumbnail. "Well, that's nice," she responded finally. She wished she could just wrap her arms around him and kiss him everywhere, but she couldn't exactly do that when he hadn't even tried to hug her hello.

Then she spied a familiar figure behind Easy and her heart started racing.

"Mr. Walsh!" crowed Angelica Pardee, Dumbarton's dorm

mistress. Angelica wasn't even thirty, but she seemed to be in a hurry to enter middle age. Today she was wearing a thin, shapeless tan cardigan, a straight, knee-length black skirt, and sensible black Easy Spirits. Her calves were a little veiny and way too bluish-white, and she wore no makeup. "Do I have to report you already?"

Easy jumped. "I'm sorry," he apologized, dazedly pressing his hand to his head, as if he had amnesia. "I haven't been here in so long, and, like, I forgot which dorm I was in." He looked across the room, directly into Callie's eyes, and she felt her arms goose-bump.

"See you later?" she finally mouthed.

He nodded ever so slightly.

"Stables?" she whispered.

"Tomorrow?" he mouthed back.

"Why not tonight?" Callie wanted to ask. But she didn't.

"Mr. *Walsh*!" Angelica practically spat, gripping the cuff of his shirt. Her face was an abnormal red.

"Okay!" Easy yelped. "I *said* I was leaving."

Angelica shook her head and ushered Easy down the hall.

Callie turned and stared out the window. The abandoned stables were where they used to go last year to fool around. Only a few students kept horses at school, so several of the stalls were always empty. She hated that she had had to suggest they meet there, and not the other way around.

Droves of freshmen lumbered up Dumbarton's steps, carrying way too much luggage. Callie noticed how overwhelmed the girls seemed. She could relate. There were so many things about boarding school that you couldn't plan for. They'd soon discover that they didn't need half their shit and that they had forgotten the really important stuff—like empty shampoo bottles to hide vodka in. She watched the throng of freshman girls part as Easy strolled down the Dumbarton steps, nodding to the new, innocent faces. God, it was hard dating such a flirt.

She put her head in her hands. It was so obvious what had gone wrong in Spain. The last night they'd spent together, she'd admitted something to Easy that was so big and so *scary* for her to say. And what had been his answer? Nothing. Silence.

Callie sighed. They'd have to talk about it tomorrow, although she hoped they'd be doing a lot more than just talking.

BennyCunningham: My brother's friend at Exeter told me there's a new girl at Waverly who's a stripper from NYC.

HeathFerro: ?!?

BennyCunningham: Yep. Some club named . . . Hen Party? Chicken Hut? Horse Stable? I think in Brooklyn? I had my cousin who lives in the Village look it up—it's the kind of place where u take it all off. Thong included.

HeathFerro: When can I meet her?

BennyCunningham: Heath, you're nasty.

HeathFerro: Don't you know it, baby!

A WAVERLY OWL SHOULD KEEP HER

GRANNY BRAS HIDDEN AT ALL TIMES.

"Right here is fine," Jenny told the cabdriver as soon as she spied the discreet maroon sign reading WAVERLY ACADEMY hanging from a tree next to a tiny, one-story brick building. Waverly wasn't far from the train station, but Jenny hadn't been able to get here fast enough.

"You sure?" The cabdriver turned around, revealing a thin beaky nose and a faded light blue Yankees cap. "Because the front office is—"

"I'm a student here," Jenny interrupted, feeling a thrill ripple through her chest as she spoke. "I know where the front office is."

The cabdriver threw up his hands in defeat. "You're the boss." Jenny handed him a twenty, stepped out of the cab, and looked around.

She was *here*. Waverly. The grass seemed greener, the trees taller, and the sky cleaner and bluer than anywhere she'd ever been before. There were lush evergreens on all sides, and on her right was a wide, cobblestone path snaking up a hill. A green field spread out to her left, and in the distance a few boys in Abercrombie fatigue shorts were kicking around a soccer ball. The whole place *smelled* of boarding school. Like the deep woods, which she'd only been in a few times, before she knew better than to accompany her dad and his kooky anarchist buddies on camping trips in southern Vermont.

A cream-colored Mercedes convertible swept past her. She heard a stately clock tower bong out one o'clock.

"Yes," she whispered, hugging herself. She had definitely arrived.

The truth was, she'd wanted to get out of the cab because she couldn't wait a second longer to plant her feet on Waverly ground, not because she knew exactly where she was going. Staring at the little brick building beside her, she realized that ivy had grown over the windows and the door was rusted shut. This definitely wasn't the front office, where she needed to check in. Another car, this one a battleship-gray Bentley, passed her. Jenny decided to follow the parade of luxury cars.

She dragged her bags up the freshly mowed hill, her kitten heels sinking into the slightly wet, springy lawn. A running track circled off to her right, flanked by tall white bleachers. A few girls were running briskly around the track, their ponytails bouncing. At the top of the hill, above the dark green trees, she could see a white church spire and the slate roofs of some more redbrick buildings. The boys with the soccer ball had stopped playing and were now standing together, staring in her direction. Were they staring at *her*?

"D'you need a ride?" a male voice interrupted her thoughts. Jenny looked over, and saw a tan, middle-aged man with dazzling white teeth hanging out the driver-side window of a silver Cadillac Escalade. She could see her reflection in his Ray-Ban aviator sunglasses. She looked awkward and silly wearing a too-tight Lacoste cotton polo shirt and dragging her luggage up the hill in a pair of pointy pink kitten-heel sandals. She'd bought the shirt at Bloomingdale's because she'd been sure it would make her feel like she absolutely belonged at boarding school, and she had gone back to visit the sandals several times before they finally went on sale so she could buy them.

"Um, sure. I'm going to the front office." She slid into the backseat of the SUV, which smelled like new car. A dirty-blond boy with chiseled features was sitting in the passenger seat looking sulky, but he didn't twist around to speak to her.

"I don't know, Heath," the man told the boy quietly. "You may not be able to have the party—your mother and I might need the Woodstock house that weekend."

"Mother*fucker*," the boy hissed under is breath. His father sighed.

Jenny barely acknowledged the boy's rudeness. She only had ears for one word: party.

She felt funny, though, asking the boy about it, since he seemed pretty pissed off. The car stopped at an enormous redbrick building with a small maroon sign next to the stone pathway that said FRONT OFFICE. Jenny squeaked her thanks, grabbed her bags, and made a beeline for the door.

Inside, the waiting room was ballroom size, with shiny floors made of dark cherry wood. A large crystal chandelier hung from the double-height ceiling. Four butter-colored leather couches were arranged in a square around a heavy teak coffee table, and a beautiful, amber-haired boy was stretched out on one of them, reading *FHM* and eating a bag of Fritos.

"Can I help you?" someone asked behind her. Jenny jumped. She turned and saw a Laura Ashley–clad older woman with a very hairsprayed gray bob and watery blue eyes wearing a name tag that read HELLO, MY NAME IS MRS. TULLINGTON sitting behind a desk with a little white sign that read NEW STUDENTS' CHECK-IN.

"Hi!" Jenny peeped. "I'm Jennifer Humphrey. I'm a new student!"

She studied the *Welcome to Waverly* schedule that was taped to the desk. School didn't officially begin until tomorrow night at the orientation welcome dinner, but sports team tryouts would take place tomorrow during the day. Mrs. Tullington typed some information into a pristine, gunmetal-gray Sony laptop, and then she frowned. "There's a problem."

Jenny stared at her blankly. *Problem?* There were no problems in magical Waverly land! Look at how gorgeous that Frito-eating boy was!

"We have you down as a boy," Mrs. Tullington continued.

"Wait, what?" Jenny snapped back to consciousness. "Did you say a *boy?*"

"Yes . . . we have you here as *Mr.* Jennifer Humphrey." The older woman seemed flustered, flipping papers back and forth. "Some students have very old family names, you see, and maybe the admissions committee thought Jennifer was—"

"Oh," Jenny replied self-consciously, twisting around to see if the boy on the couch had heard, but he was gone. All the Waverly mail she'd gotten had been addressed to a Mr. Jennifer Humphrey. She'd assumed it was just a typo. What a dumb thing to assume. *So* Old Jenny. "What does that mean? I had all my bags shipped to the . . . the Richards dorm, I think it was?"

"Yes, but that's the boys' dorm." Mrs. Tullington explained this slowly, as if Jenny didn't get it. "We'll have to find another space for you." She flipped through some papers. "The girls' dorms are all filled up. . . ." She picked up the phone. "We'll sort this out. But go see if your things are in Richards dorm. They would have been sent to the lounge on the first floor— that's where all mailed luggage is held. It's down the path to your right, fourth building. There's a sign. We'll send someone for you once we figure this out."

"Okay," Jenny replied happily, picturing all the hot, shirt-less preppy boys she was about to see lounging around Richards. "No problem."

"The main door should be open. But don't go into any of the rooms. They're off limits!" Mrs. Tullington called after her.

"Of course," Jenny agreed. "Thank you!"

Jenny stood on the stone porch of the front office. From studying the campus maps, she'd learned that Waverly's dorms, chapel, auditorium, and classrooms were all laid out in a big circle, with the soccer fields in the center. At the back of the circle were the crew houses, the Hudson River, the art gallery, the botany labs, and the library. All of the buildings seemed to be made of brick, with old, heavy windows and white trim.

Strolling excitedly toward the dorms, Jenny had to will herself not to skip. Girls in beat-up Citizens jeans and ragged grosgrain flip-flops were spilling out of Mercedes SUVs and Audi wagons, hugging other girls and talking excitedly about what had happened over the summer at their country houses on Martha's Vineyard and in the Hamptons. Boys in zip-up hooded sweatshirts and camo shorts were ramming into each other with their shoulders. One guy carrying a Louis Vuitton duffel shouted, "I did so much E this summer, my brain is fried!"

Jenny felt her body stiffen, suddenly intimidated. Everyone looked so beautiful—scrubbed and clean and fashionable without even *trying* to be, which was so much cooler than spending hours primping, like she usually did—and like they'd known one another forever. Jenny took a deep breath and continued along the path.

Then, out of nowhere, a giant potatolike thing swooped down, making a horrific cawing noise, and flew about an inch from Jenny's face.

"Aghh!" she screamed, swatting in front of her.

She watched as the thing soared into a tree. Scary! It looked like a rat on steroids.

Behind her, Jenny heard a snicker and wheeled around. All the girls were still talking to one another, but two boys in backwards W baseball caps were sitting on a stone wall, watching. Then she noticed that in her fright, she'd dropped her overpacked suitcase on the path, and it had sprung open. *Oh, God.* Her giant nude extra-support bras, the kind with the extra hook-and-eye clasp and padded straps that she had to use when she had her period, were all over the ground. They were bras a huge, dumpy grandmother might wear.

She quickly shoved the bras back in her suitcase, peeking to see if the two boys sitting on the wall had noticed. They were already greeting some other guy in a white baseball cap, doing that hand-grab half-hug thing that guys do, not paying any attention to Jenny. With the fresh air and lush, rambling scenery, maybe oversized boobs and bras weren't the kind of thing Waverly kids noticed. . . .

Then the new arrival turned to Jenny and touched the brim of his ratty white baseball cap with his index finger. He gave her a wink, as if to say, *The air might be fresh, but we're not totally blind.*

WAVERLY OWLS KNOW THAT CLEAN LUNGS MAKE FOR HEALTHY HOOTING!

Brandon Buchanan sat on one of his Samsonites and stared at Heath Ferro. No matter when he arrived on campus, he always saw Heath first. Even though they were roommates, Brandon found Heath really annoying most of the time.

"I brought a carton of smokes," Heath bragged as he unzipped his black medium-size Tumi duffel and showed Brandon the edge of the Camel "unfiltered" box. They were in Richards' lounge, waiting to get room assignments. It was just a normal common room—the meeting spot where the guys watched *SportsCenter*, shared sausage pizzas from Ritoli's, and flirted with cute girls during visiting hour—but still, the lounge felt English and regal. The cream-colored plaster ceilings were fifteen feet high, with dark wooden beams, and there were comfortable, worn leather armchairs scattered all over the place. An old cabinet TV that got three network stations and, randomly, ESPN, loomed in the corner. On the floor lay a huge, ornate Oriental carpet. Careless cigarette burn holes made the rug look even more historic.

"That'll last you about a week," Brandon scoffed, pushing his short wavy golden-brown hair back into its deliberately tousled place. Heath smoked like a fiend right outside Richards even though smoking was forbidden on campus, but the faculty constantly looked the other way. It might've been because of Heath's stunning good looks—he was tall, lean, and athletic, with gold-flecked green eyes, sharp cheekbones, and shaggy dark blond hair. But more likely, it was Heath's family that kept him out of trouble. Heath's father had donated four and a half million dollars for the Olympic-size natatorium and another million for a three-floor addition to the renovated botany library, so Heath could pretty much do as he damn well pleased and never get so much as a warning.

"You bring your weird girly cream with you this year?" Heath teased.

"It's moisturizer," Brandon clarified.

"It's moisturizer," Heath echoed in a high-pitched voice.

So what if Brandon took good care of his skin? And liked nice clothes and shoes and liked his wavy hair to be just so? He was neurotic about his height—he was only five-eight—and shaved his chest because he hated the tiny little hairs that grew in the caved-in part of his breastbone. His less-clean friends busted on him to no end. But so what?

"Who you think they're gonna room us with?" Heath asked.

"Don't know. Maybe Ryan. Unless he gets a single again."
Ryan Reynolds's father had invented the soft contact lens and
openly used his wealth as leverage to his son's advantage. Lots
of kids' parents bribed the school, but usually it was kept a
secret.

Heath snickered. "Maybe you'll get paired up with Walsh."

"Nah, even the administration knows better than that,"
Brandon replied. Just the sound of that name—Walsh, as in
Easy Walsh—made Brandon's blood curdle.

"So, how's Natasha?" Heath recited her name with a bad
Russian accent.

Brandon sighed. Last April he had started going out with
Natasha Wood, who went to Millbrook Academy, after Easy
stole his old girlfriend, Callie Vernon, from him. "We broke up
two weeks ago."

"No shit. You cheat?"

"Nah."

"What, then?"

Brandon shrugged. They'd broken up because he was still
moony over Callie. He and Natasha had been making out on
the Harwich main beach in Cape Cod, and Brandon had acci-
dentally called Natasha Callie by mistake. Oops. Natasha had
climbed up the rickety wooden lifeguard stand and refused to
come down until Brandon went away. Forever.

"Whose stuff is that?" Heath looked across the room and
kicked his feet up on the brown tweed couch. There was a
whole pile of bright pink canvas L.L. Bean bags that didn't have
an owner yet.

Brandon shrugged. "Don't know." He picked up one of the tags. "'Jennifer Humphrey.'"

"There's going to be a guy named Jennifer Humphrey in this dorm? Freaky."

"No, *I'm* Jennifer."

A little curly-haired girl in a sweet light purple Marc Jacobs knockoff skirt stood in the common-room doorway. Brandon knew the skirt was a knockoff, because he'd bought Natasha the real deal this summer. This Jennifer had a tiny upturned nose and pink cheeks and wore little skinny-heeled pink shoes with tiny cut-outs at the front so he could just glimpse her toes peeking through.

"Hi," she said simply.

"Uh," Brandon stammered. "You're not . . . supposed to be—"

"No . . . actually . . . I am." She laughed a little. "I was assigned to this dorm."

"So you're *Mister* Jennifer Humphrey?"

**Will Jenny's dreams of reinventing herself
come true at Waverly?**

Find out how far one girl will go to be . . .

Read the whole novel, available now.